Angie Lake

The Farts of Gratitude

Published by Sweet Cherry Publishing Limited
Unit 36, Vulcan House
Vulcan Road
Leicester, LE5 3EF
United Kingdom

www.sweetcherrypublishing.com

First published in the UK in 2019
ISBN: 978-1-78226-263-3

2 4 6 8 10 9 7 5 3 1

Danny Dingle's Fantastic Finds: The Farts of Gratitude

Printed and bound in India

DANNY DINGLE'S

FANTASTIC FINDS

Book 5

The Farts of Gratitude

Written by Angie Lake

DANNY DiNGLE'S SUPER-SECRET SPY NOTEBOOK.

ABSOLUTELY DO NOT READ (unless you are Danny, Percy or Superdog).

NOTE: If you are not Danny, Percy or Superdog . . .

A **HUGE** blob of snot will get stuck to your hand as soon as you turn the page.

URRGHH!!!!!

TOLD YOU SO!

Allow me to introduce myself, although you have probably heard of me and my fantastic inventions.

My name is Danny Dingle. Though you may know me by my superhero identity:

EXPERIMENTAL FACE!!!

. . . No? . . . What do you mean you've never heard of **EXPERIMENTAL FACE?**

. . . You know . . . **EXPERIMENTAL FACE!!!**

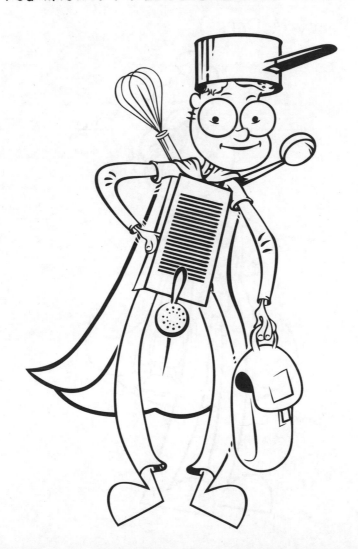

I have a trusty sidekick, the mysterious **Brass Invader!** (He's really my best friend, classifier of fantastic finds and assistant in general, Percy McDuff.)

Now, this particular inventor's notebook is slightly different to my other ones: as I write I'm returning from a **TOP-SECRET** reconnaissance mission in Spain.

What was I doing in Spain, I hear you ask? Well, I can't tell you. As I said, it was **TOP SECRET**. But I can tell you that, in order to remain ~~insonspc~~, ~~enconspicuo~~ . . . in order to go unnoticed, Percy and I thought it best to disguise the mission as a family holiday.

It's a bit of a long story, but Percy and I took part in this competitive **SPY TRAINING** exercise where we had to build a flying machine. We successfully completed this stage of the training and passed onto the next stage, which is the **SECRET RECONAISSANCE MISSION IN SPAIN.** (Or Operation Family Holiday, as we've been calling it for reasons of secrecy.)

The fact that the mission or "prize" was for just one family did cause a bit of tension between my parents and Percy's parents. There was quite a lot of arguing about which family went on "holiday" with us:

It wasn't an easy decision. First Percy's dad tried begging:

But my dad responded with a song:

In the meantime our mums were holding negotiations of their own:

POINT 1755: BOTH BOYS TO BE PICKED UP FROM JIU-JITSU EVERY WEEK.

Eventually, after all negotiations failed, our dads decided to settle things the old-fashioned way: by filling a paddling pool with baked beans and wrestling each other in it in the back garden.

Dad **LOST**. All the neighbours were there, so it was pretty EMBARRASSING.

Mum was not happy about having to take us on the trip to Spain . . . or about all the baked beans in the back garden. Although she did say that the money from the ticket sales of the 'Dads in Beans' wrestling match would come in handy as spending money for the holiday.

Percy and I were just glad that the argument had been settled. We had far more IMPORTANT things to worry about, like locating Metal Face (the world's most incredibly fartastic superhero) and getting the instructions for our top-secret mission.

We knew that Metal Face had top-secret business in Spain and we were to meet him there for new instructions. He mentioned it that time we bumped into him outside the toilets at that sci-fi convention.

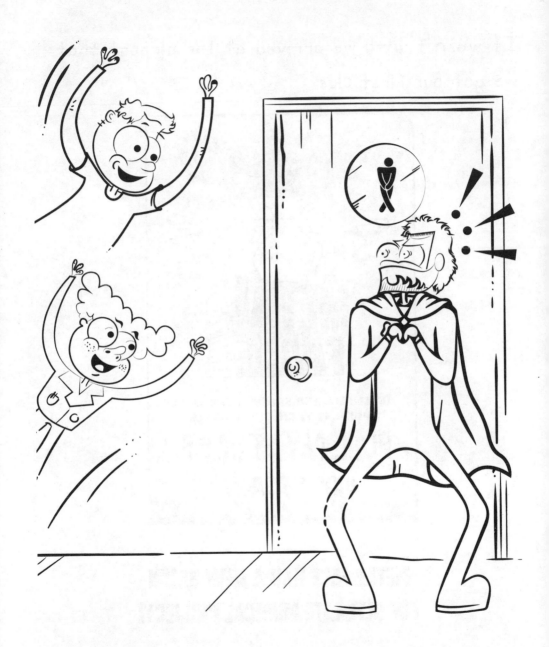

It wasn't until we arrived at the airport that we got our first clue:

METAL FACE HAD A NEW BAND!
THE ULTIMATE MUSICAL PROJECT!

Metal Face's band was called **Gross Awful Gasses**. (GAG for short.) They had just released an album, the appropriately named FARTASMATRON, and their first single had gone straight to number 64 in the charts! Percy and I put some money together and we bought the hit song 'Pull my Finger'.

It was the most AWESOME song ever!

We knew the song must contain some super-secret coded information, so we went to painstaking trouble to learn every part of it.

It started with a MASSIVE FART then lots of other farts. Percy and I listened to the song over and over again, singing along to it in the airport . . .

On the plane . . .

Dad started singing along in the car . . .

Mum dropped us off at the Iberia Eleganza
Hotel . . .

. . . and we kept singing during the long walk to the Crab View Hotel. (The hotel that we were actually staying at.)

The song went like this:

I WILL BLOW YOUR MIND
WITH MY AWESOME BEHIND
AND MY BUM WILL EXPLODE
WITH GAS THAT WILL CORRODE
WHEN YOU PULL MY FINGER!
WE DON'T HAVE MUCH TIME
BEFORE THIS FART OF MINE
KNOCKS YOU OVER, DUDE
COS I HAD MEXICAN FOOD
COME ON PULL MY FINGER!
YOU'LL TREMBLE IN THE WAKE
OF A HUGE FARTQUAKE
I LIVE ON EGGS AND SPROUTS
YOU'RE ABOUT TO FIND OUT
WHEN YOU PULL MY FINGER!
YOU'D BETTER START TO RUN
YOU'RE GONNA FEEL THE SUM
OF DINNER YESTERDAY
AT THE BAKED BEAN BUFFET
OH WHEN YOU PULL MY FINGER!

27

Anyway, Mum hadn't been very happy with us all day. I think she was still cross with us about the "airport incident".

When Percy, Dad and I arrived at the right hotel (the Crab View), Percy and I went straight upstairs to unpack Superdog.
Who or what is this Superdog, I hear you cry? Superdog is the greatest genius, the most talented inventor, the BRAINS of our entire operation . . . my FARTABULOUS TELEPATHIC PET TOAD!!!

NO.1 INVENTOR!

SUPERHERO!

GENIUS!

TELEPATH!

EXTRAORDINARY!

Mum didn't want him to come on holiday with us, but I couldn't leave him behind with such an IMPORTANT mission ahead. I put him very carefully in a plastic container, and then I punched holes in the top of the container so that he wouldn't suffocate.

It then occurred to me that I'd better poke a few air holes in the suitcase too. I opened the packed case and put Superdog's box in the middle so that it would be cushioned by all the clothes. I closed the case, then I DRILLED HOLES all over the suitcase so that Superdog would get plenty of oxygen.

GENIUS

Fortunately, Superdog had survived the trip just fine. **UNFORTUNATELY**, it had been a bit of a bumpy ride and Superdog had been a bit sick. Okay, quite a lot sick. **AND** he'd rolled around in it. **AND** a lot of the sick had leaked out through the air holes onto the clothes in the suitcase, along with the dead flies and beetles that I packed for Superdog's lunch.

So I guess that it was probably for the best that I'd decided to borrow Dad's suitcase to smuggle Superdog into the country. I mean I couldn't possibly have used my own case . . . where would I have put all the fart potion?

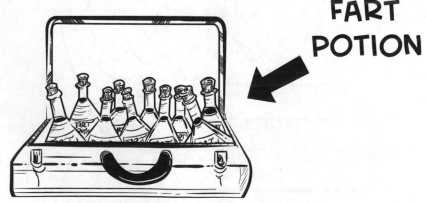

FART POTION

Anyway, all the toad sick and dead beetles made Percy VERY sick. Luckily I managed to get Dad's suitcase in front of him and I caught all the sick in that. We decided it was better to leave before anything else happened, so we put Dad's suitcase away and went back to our own room.

Percy and I are inventors, after all. Just because we were on a ~~covert top-secret mission~~ **HOLIDAY** was no excuse for not making something **AWESOME** out of fantastic holiday finds.

We had been very careful to pack our special inventors' kits that we carry around with us at all times. The kits consist of:

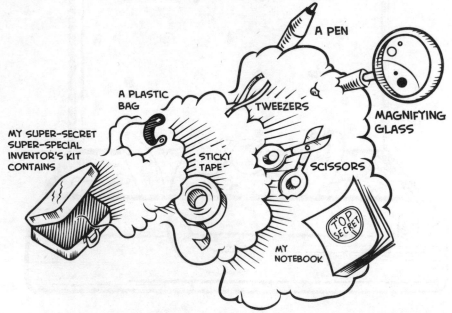

A PEN

MAGNIFYING GLASS

A PLASTIC BAG

TWEEZERS

MY SUPER-SECRET SUPER-SPECIAL INVENTOR'S KIT CONTAINS

STICKY TAPE

SCISSORS

MY NOTEBOOK

TOP SECRET

But as we were going to be away in a mysterious foreign land, Percy and I decided to bring a few extra things with us in our hand luggage:

A HAMMER

A SOLDERING IRON AND SOLDER

A GLUE GUN

TWO BRICKS

A SET OF SCREWDRIVERS

VARIOUS JAM JARS AND TINS CONTAINING NAILS, SCREWS, PAPER CLIPS, RUBBER BANDS

Unfortunately we had to leave a few things behind to be able to fit all this stuff in the case. (Percy's clothes, our beach towels, the shampoo, toothpaste . . . all of our toiletries, really.)

It was a bit of a surprise when the bag was confiscated as we were going through security: apparently a lot of those things aren't allowed on planes . . .

Anyway, the whole family was stopped. Mum and Dad were asked to go into a little office for questioning.

And that was the "airport incident" I mentioned earlier.

Mum and Dad were eventually released, but our hand luggage was CONFISCATED. It looked like we'd have to improvise without these things . . . and Percy would have to improvise without clothes.

Fortunately Mum hadn't mentioned "the incident" since we arrived at the Crab View Hotel and I wasn't about to say or do anything that might remind her about it. Percy and I were on a mission. We had far more important things to do than get into petty arguments with my mum about who nearly got who arrested.

Percy and I grabbed what was left of our **iNVENTORS' KiTS** and went down to the terrace and pool area to see what fantastic finds we could make. We looked under sunbeds, in bins and behind bushes and we made the following

FANTASTIC FiNDS:

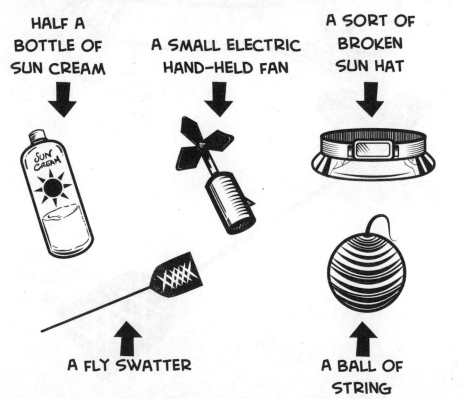

HALF A
BOTTLE OF
SUN CREAM

A SMALL ELECTRIC
HAND-HELD FAN

A SORT OF
BROKEN
SUN HAT

A FLY SWATTER

A BALL OF
STRING

What can you make with all that, I hear you ask? **BEHOLD**:

The sun hat with automatic sun cream application!

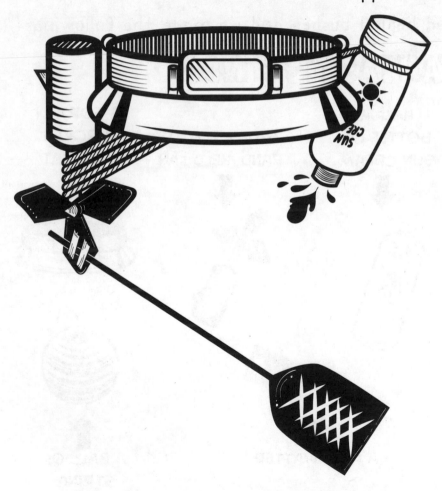

Anyway, after settling in at the Crab View Hotel and after building the fartabulous sun hat with sun cream applicator (patent pending), the hotel pool was temporarily closed to the public because a toad (that we know **NOTHING** about) was seen floating on the pool on a lilo eating an ice cream . . .

We decided we wanted a change of scenery anyway, so we found Mum and Dad and insisted that what they needed was a relaxing afternoon on the beach. The hotel manager had started QUESTIONING some of the guests, so Percy and I decided to get Mum and Dad out of there quickly before they heard anything Superdog-related.

LET'S GO TO THE BEACH!

43

I grabbed Superdog before Mum and Dad could see him and hid him in my inventor's bag. Obviously there wasn't room for my kit in there now, so Percy had to carry mine along with his.

I'd changed into my beach shorts and flip-flops, Dad had changed into some holey shorts that smelt of SICK (toad and human) and Percy hadn't changed as he didn't have any clothes to change into.

We got into the car with Mum and Mel. Mum nagged Dad all the way to the beach about his mangled clothes:

OH YES, JAMES! IT HAPPENS ALL THE TIME: VANDALS STEAL YOUR SUITCASE, VOMIT ON YOUR CLOTHES AND THEN PUT EVERYTHING BACK WITHOUT STEALING ANYTHING . . .

MAYBE SOMEONE TOOK DAD'S SUITCASE, BUT WHEN THEY SAW THAT DAD DIDN'T HAVE ANYTHING WORTH STEALING THEY WERE SICK IN IT . . . YOU KNOW, AS REVENGE . . .

47

Anyway, we drove around for ages and ages because it was impossible to park. Eventually we found a space and made our way onto the beach, which was jam packed.

Mum set up her parasol and settled down to play with Mel. Dad went straight into the sea to see if he could wash the smell of SICK off his shorts.

Percy and I went looking for some fantastic beach finds.

We went up to some rock pools at one end of the beach where we found lots and lots of crabs.

I realised that an army of well-trained crabs with cameras stuck to their backs could make a valuable addition to our team, and would allow us to infiltrate all kinds of high-security locations.

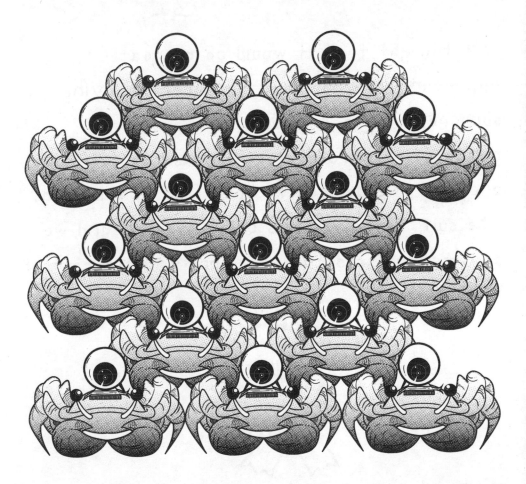

When we got back to our parasol Mum had gone for a walk with Mel, and Dad (who had been left in charge of watching over all our belongings) had fallen fast asleep.

We thought that it would be a great opportunity to try out our super-spraying, sun cream-spreading sun hat (patent pending). In order to really test it out properly, we decided to bury Dad in the sand. The sun hat only works on your face, and we didn't want Dad to get sunburn on the rest of his body.

GENIUS

Percy, Superdog, and I VERY CAREFULLY buried Dad under a big pile of sand. Then we put the sun hat on Dad's head and turned it on before going to put the bucket of crabs in the car to train later. Then we returned to the beach to make more **FANTASTIC FINDS**.

After about an hour we couldn't really find much else of interest apart from sand and seaweed, so we went back to the parasol. Dad was NOT happy. Apparently the sun hat had suffered a **SLIGHT MALFUNCTION**. For the past hour it had squirted sun cream in his eyes whilst the fly swatter went round and round, slapping him repeatedly in the face until the battery ran out.

Despite his injuries, Dad had to admit that it was a **pretty good invention**. He vowed to make a few adjustments and try it on Mum when she fell asleep.

Percy and I dug Dad out of his sand prison, then Mum came back and suggested we go back to the hotel, get changed and go for dinner.

Percy, Mel, Superdog and I got into the back of the car. Percy and I were determined to keep singing 'Pull my Finger' until our throats were sore or until Mum's head exploded (whichever happened first).

At this point, Dad looked down at his feet. I don't think he should have screamed or started shaking his legs about. The crabs that were climbing up his legs got very nervous and started pinching him, which made him scream and shake even more, which made the crabs more nervous . . .

We had completely forgotten about the bucket we had left under the seat. Percy and I shared a look. Clearly this was not a good time to mention our plans to train up a CRAB ARMY (they were already pretty good fighters). It was very hard for anyone to concentrate in those circumstances anyway. The crabs remained the centre of everyone's attention until the car DROVE THROUGH the front window of an ice cream shop.

Although Mum and Dad weren't happy about the ice cream shop incident, it was a very fortunate twist of fate. If Dad hadn't **CRASHED** into the ice cream shop causing hundreds of pounds worth of damage, we wouldn't have seen THE POSTER!

WHAT POSTER?

Only the poster announcing that in the town of Benifarty on that very night, Metal Face and the **Gross Awful Gasses** would be performing live at a big, free, open-air festival . . .

IT WAS THE SECOND CLUE!!!

Percy looked at me stunned, and then put his head to one side. Hundreds and thousands started pouring out of his ear. I took the wafer out of my nose and said:

DO YOU KNOW WHAT THIS MEANS, PERCY?

...THE ICE CREAM IN OUR HAIR?

NO, NOT THAT! THE POSTER, THE CONCERT...IT'S THE SECOND CLUE! IT'S OUR MISSION, DON'T YOU SEE? WE HAVE TO GET TO THAT CONCERT TONIGHT SO WE CAN GET OUR INSTRUCTIONS FROM METAL FACE HIMSELF!

Percy's eyes widened as he realised that this was part of our mission . . . and also as he caught a glimpse of himself in a mirror and saw how ridiculous he looked.

We looked at each other knowingly. Percy and I knew we had some serious sucking up to do if we wanted Mum to agree to us going to the concert, especially after the ice cream shop incident, which Mum was bound to think was somehow MY FAULT. (She always blames me for these things.) Whilst Dad was settling the insurance claim with the shop, we decided to write her a song. It was time to commence **Operation GAG**!

The first part of the operation involved using my ADVANCED PERSUASION TECHNIQUES:

Danny: If we can go to the concert I promise I'll get As in every subject.

Mum: Danny, you've failed almost everything year after year. Your only chance of passing everything is if you invent some sort of magic helmet that brainwashes your teachers into passing you!

(Note to self: Invent a magic brainwashing helmet.)

Danny: Okay, I promise that I'll clean the whole house every day . . .

Mum: I don't think so. I wasn't impressed the last time, when you got your dad to turbo charge the vacuum cleaner and it sucked all the wallpaper off the walls.

Danny: What about if I promise that I'll go back to Jiu-Jitsu?

Mum: Hang on a minute, what do you mean go back to Jiu-Jitsu? You're still enrolled in Jiu-Jitsu . . . I'm still paying for it.

 . . . OOOPS!!! Looks like I forgot to tell Mum that Percy and I had stopped going to Jiu-Jitsu so we could spend more time in our secret laboratory **CLUBHOUSE** learning the art of telepathy from Superdog.

Danny: Oh, yeah . . . I mean I'll keep going back next year too . . .

Bribery wasn't working. It became clear that a song was going to be the only solution:

OH MUMMY DARLING, AT SEVEN IT STARTS
  IT'S MORE THAN A CONCERT;
    IT'S MORE THAN JUST CULTURE
      IT'S CULTURE WITH FARTS
  OH MUMMY DEAREST, WHY CAN'T YOU SEE?
FOR GROSS AWFUL GASSES I'D PASS ALL MY CLASSES
          YES, EVEN P.E.

    OH MUMMY DARLING, PLEASE KEEP IN MIND
  I NEED SOME MOTIVATION AS SCHOOL IS JUST DULL
        AND I'M FALLING BEHIND . . .
      AND TONIGHT WILL BE A CELEBRATION
  OF FARTING, DIARRHOEA AND EVEN CONSTIPATION
    OH MUMMY DARLING, AT SEVEN IT STARTS . . .

Then Dad joined in:

OH GWEN MY DARLING,
DON'T BE A FOOL
I'LL TAKE ALL THE KIDS
AND YOU CAN JUST REST
WITH A BOOK BY THE POOL

Mum seemed happy with the deal. Dad said that he was "super hyped to have the chance to see GAG performing 'Pull my Finger' live".

The concert was absolutely **AWESOME** and it was really crowded. Fortunately I'd remembered to bring a few bottles of Dad's pickled eel and mustard fart potion, so no one stood anywhere near us and we managed to get quite a good view.

Percy and I were thrilled to see GAG live, but not as thrilled as Dad who was almost crying with joy. It didn't help that he had insisted on wearing the super-squirter sun hat. He had made a few **MODIFICATIONS** to it so that he didn't get slapped in the face quite as often and the sun cream wasn't being squirted directly into his eyes anymore. It was being squirted onto his forehead and running down his face, so a lot of it was still going into his eyes . . . but he insisted that he was crying tears of joy.

Dad: This is the best concert I've been to in years . . .

Danny: Dad, isn't this the ONLY concert you've been to in years?

When the concert was over we went right up to the stage to see if we could speak to Metal Face and get our instructions. (And an autograph!) We squeezed through the crowd and found a place just by the steps at the side of the stage. When the band came down the steps, I could see that Metal Face looked very different from the last few times I'd seen him. This time he was quite a lot taller and more muscular, with long blond hair.

This just goes to show what a true master of disguise he is!!!

GENIUS

Metal Face actually stopped to talk to us! He looked straight at us, then completely blanked Percy and me as if he'd never seen us before. Obviously he did this so he wouldn't blow our cover. Instead he went up to Dad.

Metal Face: Hey there, nice hat! (He said pointing at Dad's AWESOME sun squirter hat)

Dad: My son made it . . . well, with help from his friend . . .

Metal Face: Oh . . . Well, it's definitely something you don't see every day.

Danny: Mr Metal Face, Your Highness . . . could you tell us about your mission?

Metal Face: Well . . . our mission is to rock out, right? To get everybody rockin'! YEAH!!!!

Danny: Okay, I understand. Don't worry, the mission is in safe hands.

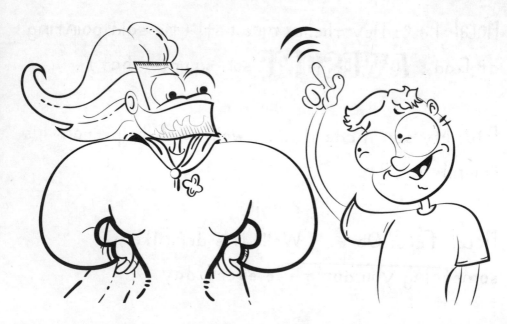

Dad asked Metal Face to give us his autograph, then he searched his pockets for something to give him as a gift before handing over the super-squirter sun hat.

Metal Face looked at it in awe.

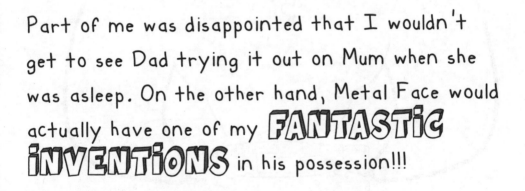

Part of me was disappointed that I wouldn't get to see Dad trying it out on Mum when she was asleep. On the other hand, Metal Face would actually have one of my **FANTASTIC INVENTIONS** in his possession!!!

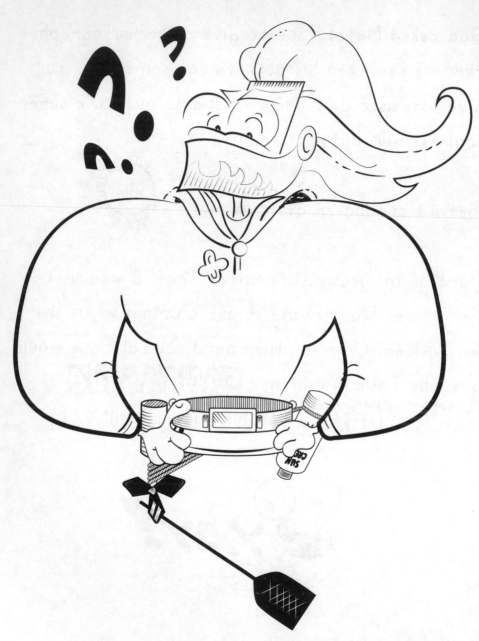

Metal Face: Well, thanks for that . . . I'm sure there's nothing else like it anywhere in the world!

We would have kept talking, but Metal Face was escorted rapidly away from the stage. I assume he had lots of **SUPERHERO** business to take care of.

I turned to Percy and looked at him knowingly.

Danny: Mission accomplished!

Percy: Yes!!! Err . . . what?

Danny: What do you mean, what? Don't you see? **WE HAVE TO GET EVERYBODY TO ROCK OUT!**

Danny: That's our mission . . . those are our instructions . . . don't you understand? Metal Face needs us to go back home and start a band that sings about farting so that we can get everybody to rock out!

Our ~~top-secret~~ ~~reconnaissance mission~~
HOLIDAY had been an overwhelming success!
And, thanks to Dad, Metal Face now has one
of my fantastic inventions, so I'm much, much
closer to achieving my lifelong dream of going
to work for him one day in his secret lair helping
him invent . . . well . . . inventions.

Anyway, we decided to make our way back to the hotel, but on the way out of the stadium we saw a merchandise stand selling t-shirts and records, so Dad insisted on buying the whole Fartasmatron album to listen to in the car. He also got us all **Gross Awful Gasses** t-shirts! Percy was especially delighted as he didn't have anything else to wear.

That was by far the best part of the "holiday". For the next two weeks we did beachy holiday-type stuff to try to blend in with the other tourists. We didn't want to give ourselves away as superheroes on a top-secret mission, after all.

WE BUILT A
GIGANTIC
SANDCASTLE
(IN THE HOTEL ROOM)

WE TOOK A
BOAT RIDE
(STOWED AWAY IN THE
LIFEBOAT OF A CRUISE
SHIP TO MOROCCO)

CAN WE GET
OFF NOW?

WE ATE OUT AT RESTAURANTS
(AT ONE POINT WE THOUGH SUPERDOG WAS GOING TO BLOW IS COVER)

During those two weeks Dad, Percy and I went everywhere in our **Gross Awful Gasses** t-shirts. At first Mum was really annoyed, but after the first week she got over it and was just really embarrassed.

It's been a ~~successful mission~~ **REALLY FUN HOLIDAY**, but I think everyone is keen to get back home (especially Mum).

Percy and I can't wait to go back to school! Everyone is going to be so impressed that we've discovered Metal Face's **AWESOME** new band and seen them live. I can just imagine how jealous they'll be that Metal Face came to meet me. Especially when I tell them that he was so impressed with my fartabulous super-squirter sun hat that he just had to meet the **GENIUS** behind it.

GENIUS

We're going to wear our **GAG** t-shirts and spread the word about Metal Face's band! Percy and I spent ages last night practising our harmonies for when we sing 'Pull My Finger' in front of everyone.

As it turned out, everyone had heard the song. Quite a lot of the kids in class had seen **GAG** over the summer as they had been performing all over Europe.

Everyone in school was completely obsessed with the band. There wasn't a notebook or binder that didn't have a **GAG** logo doodled on it.

Oh well! At least everyone was really impressed that Percy and I had become CLOSE FRIENDS with Metal Face and that I had single-handedly saved him from terminal sunburn with my fartabulous super-squirter sun hat.

GAG became the subject of every conversation. Miss Quimby seemed pretty sick of reading about it though:

GEOGRAPHY TEST

1. WRITE ABOUT THE CAPITAL OF ITALY

Rome, the capital of Italy, was the third city visited by
— GROSS AWFUL GASSES —
on their European tour...

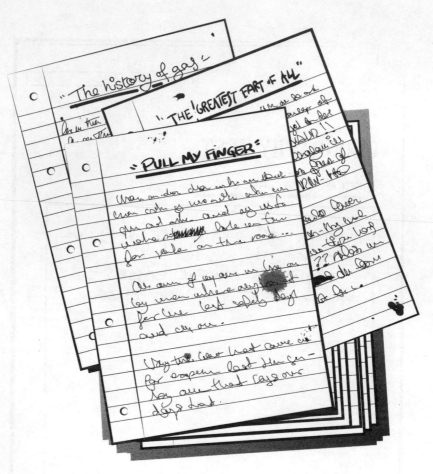

She seemed to be eating even more DOUGHNUTS than usual. She banned any fart-related work and essays could not be handed in in song format, nor could the theme be 'Pull my Finger'.

Anyway, we had P.E. in the afternoon with the fearsome, scaresome, **TERRIFYING** Ms Mills.

I swear that she just gets scarier every year. Everyone thinks so. **ESPECIALLY** Mr Hammond, our science teacher. Ms Mills has been trying to get Mr Hammond to go out with her for years, and Percy and I have sort of been trying to help in any way possible. (Mainly because if we give Ms Mills information about Mr Hammond we get away with not doing any actual exercise during P.E. class. We don't **PASS** exactly . . . but at least we can get through without making any effort.)

Unfortunately Ms Mills hasn't been helping herself much. A few weeks ago she attacked Mr Hammond during the **ROBOT RIOT** finals and he had to be rescued by Granny Jean. So Mr Hammond has been avoiding her even more than usual, which means Ms Mills has been even more

miserable than usual . . . and P.E. class has been
more like boot camp than usual.

Anyway, for today's P.E. class we'd been told
to bring our bikes to school for a road safety
training bike ride, so there would be no getting
out of SOME exercise.

Fortunately Percy and I knew how to get out of
most of it. Let me explain:

1) The road safety training route always leaves
the school via the main gate, then turns right.

2) There's a nice downhill street that ends at
Edmund Road before we pass the sweet shop and
take another right.

3) Just before we go around the corner, Percy and I start lagging behind, just enough to let the whole group turn the corner and head towards the park . . .

4) . . . where they'll cycle around the lake before taking . . .

5) . . . the bike path uphill towards the school.

It takes them 40 minutes to get back again. It takes us 40 minutes, too: 30 minutes to walk around the sweet shop and 10 minutes to push our bikes to an alley just by the school where we wait to join onto the end of the group.

Unfortunately Ms Mills didn't turn right at Edmund Street. Instead she kept going and going. We rode past the **sweet shop**, down the high street, past the supermarket and up a little residential road. We stopped at Number 5, Windsor Road. That's where Ms Mills told us to get off our bikes.

RIGHT, KIDS!
FITNESS CLUB CHALLENGE! I WANT YOU TO RUSH AROUND THE GARDEN, LOOK EVERYWHERE, LEAVE NO STONE UNTURNED AND NOTE DOWN AS MUCH INFORMATION AS YOU CAN ABOUT THIS HOUSE AND GARDEN!

IS THIS LEGAL?

IS THIS MR HAMMOND'S HOUSE?

We spent a good hour looking around the garden. We wrote down how many plants he has in his front garden, what kind of curtains he has, what colour the garage door is painted . . .

Percy: What should I do, Danny?

Danny: Stop following me around! Go and count the stones in the driveway or something.

Percy: Okay!

He pretends like he doesn't, but Percy loves counting things . . . it's one of his duties when he catalogues our **FANTASTIC FINDS**.

P.E. turned out to be quite fun! It was pretty good spy training, and way better than doing any real exercise.

But I've been thinking . . . getting an A in P.E. by getting Mr Hammond to agree to go out with Ms Mills might be an impossible mission, even for a world-class superhero such as myself. And I really need to pass PE. I promised Mum I'd pass something if she let me go to the **GAG** gig, and **EXPERIMENTAL FACE** is a man of his word.

But the chances of getting Mr Hammond to go out with Ms Mills . . . it's just never going to happen, especially after the Robot Riot assault! HOWEVER, passing PE, even if it's just scraping through, by getting Ms Mills a boyfriend . . . **ANY BOYFRIEND** . . . now, that could be an idea!

What we need is a special spy mission, the nature of which will be discussed secretly, in a secret discussion with Percy and Superdog in the Super Secret Spy Club later. **SECRETLY. IN SECRET.**

Percy, Superdog and I met after school for our secret meeting.

The plan was as follows:

1) The Mission: to pass P.E. by getting Ms Mills a boyfriend.

2) Get as much background information on Ms Mills as possible.

3) Find an appropriate dating website for Ms Mills and begin **OPERATION FABFART** (Find A Boyfriend For A Repulsive Teacher).

Percy and I agreed that we'd need to carry out our research the next time Ms Mills wasn't home, so the next day in P.E. class we took the opportunity to gather some intelligence:

Danny: So, Ms Mills . . . do you have any plans for tonight?

Ms Mills: I was thinking of going for a walk with Mr Hammond . . .

Danny: Really? . . . Does Mr Hammond know about that?

Ms Mills: Well, we'll be going for a walk at the same time, in the same place . . .

Percy: Isn't that technically called stalking?

Ms Mills: Do you two want something?

Danny: No, no . . . just taking an interest in your life, Ms Mills.

This was **AWESOME** news! Ms Mills was going to be out for hours! This would give us hours to carry out our reconnaissance mission.

It would be all too easy: all we had to do was wait for her to finish her Jiu-Jitsu class, then follow her home.

Then when she went for her walk, Percy and I would be able to snoop around her garden and find out as much secret information on Ms Mills as possible, just like Ms Mills had asked us to do with Mr Hammond.

Percy and I followed Ms Mills home in the afternoon then waited for her to go out. As Percy and I weren't new to spy training we brought a few supplies with us:

- X-RAY SPECS, BORROWED FROM DAD

- NIGHT-VISION GOGGLES, BORROWED FROM GRANDAD

- BAKED BEAN AND LEMON CURD SANDWICHES, BANNED FROM THE HOUSE BY MUM

Percy and I waited in a nearby hedge eating our sandwiches until she went out, then we were able to get a closer look at her house. We were very lucky that she left the curtains open and all the lights on when she left, so we didn't need the X-ray specs to see into her living room.

We didn't find anything too surprising, but we discovered the following about Ms Mills from the photos and trophies in her living room:

- SHE LIKES MARTIAL ARTS AND IS A JIU-JITSU INSTRUCTOR (she's our Jiu-Jitsu instructor, so we had reason to suspect this)

- SHE TEACHES P.E. AT GREENVILLE ELEMENTARY (no surprises there!)

- SHE IS IN THE TERRITORIAL ARMY (I always suspected this, because she always seems to be going to Territorial Army meetings)

ALSO:

- SHE GOES PAINTBALLING AT THE WEEKENDS

- SHE WAS SCHOOL SHOTPUT CHAMPION

With all this information, plus a photo we snapped of her when she was coming out of the school toilets, I think we have everything we need to get Ms Mills a boyfriend! YAY!

The first thing we had to do when we got home was find a **dating** website, which was not something Percy or I had much experience with.

It turns out that there are lots of dating websites out there! How were we supposed to choose?

WHY DON'T WE JOIN THEM ALL? THEN WE CAN SET HER UP WITH THE FIRST PERSON THAT SENDS HER A MESSAGE. PROBLEM SOLVED.

I was clearly very clever.

WHAT IF SHE HATES HIM? PE IS AWFUL WHEN MS MILLS IS IN A BAD MOOD.

Percy had a point.

I had another think.

We had to come up with a good boyfriend. A boyfriend so **AWESOME** that there was **NO WAY** Ms Mills could hate him. Someone so **PERFECT** she would immediately fall in love and forget all about Mr Hammond.

I'VE GOT IT! METAL FACE!!!

I admit it. I'm a genius.

BUT IF MS MILLS IS METAL FACE'S WIFE, SHE'LL MAKE HIM DO PE AND JIU-JITSU ALL THE TIME AND HE WON'T HAVE TIME FOR HIS EXTRA-SECRET MISSIONS ANYMORE.

Percy was **CLEARLY** wrong. He always is. But still, he got me thinking . . . what if Metal Face didn't like Ms Mills?

Or worse still, what if Metal Face was faced with the dilemma of choosing between going out with Ms Mills and a life of swashbuckling **superhero** adventures and saving the world?

Ms Mills wouldn't stand
a chance, it would all
end in tears, and Percy
and I would be back at
boot camp.

I KNOW! WE'LL LOOK FOR A
DATING SITE FOR PEOPLE WHO ARE
ALMOST AS AWESOME AS METAL
FACE, BUT MORE DESPERATE.

We looked up 'Metal Face dating'. We didn't
find a Metal Face dating website, but there was
a **METAL PLACE** dating website. We figured
that would be close enough.

The next thing we had to do was make a profile for Ms Mills. Okay, personal details:

Okay, let's see . . .

Name: Ms Mills

Age: . . .

We uploaded Ms Mills' photo to her profile and prepared for the next phase of **OPERATION FABFART**.

Now all we can do is wait for the messages to start rolling in. Percy and I agreed that I'll do the first shift, and if there are too many, I'll call Percy for backup. It's going to be quite a mission. I really hope it doesn't get in the way of my maths homework . . .

The next morning at school, Miss Quimby seemed very excited as she was eating her morning DOUGHNUT.

Miss Quimby: Now class, settle down, I have some big news!

I looked around. Everyone seemed pretty settled down already. I suspected that half the class may even have still been asleep.

Miss Quimby continued, 'Mr Norton, the other teachers and I have discussed how interested you all are in bands and music, so we've decided to enter our school into 'This School Has Talent', the famous TV show!!'

I prodded Percy. This sounded interesting.

You will need to come up with an ACT you can perform on the show. This will be your project for the term, so we'll spend this morning watching a few episodes to give you an idea of what you have to aim for. The producers will want to find the next BIG THING, so make it as spectacular as you can!

Everyone in the class cheered. This would be **a hundred times better** than spending all morning doing any real work! And starting a band as a project? That was a million times better than doing homework!

We all watched with interest. I could hear the other kids whispering to each other and talking about their ideas. I kept quiet: I already had a fartastic idea for a band, and I wasn't about to tell anyone about it!

'This School Has Talent' turned out
to be all that we spoke about all day. In
assembly Mr Norton told us all that he
wanted the **whole school** to be involved: from
making sets, to performing and organising
the whole event.

And in Science Club Mr Hammond seemed full of
ideas, some good . . .

THIS IS A GREAT OPPORTUNITY
FOR ALL OF YOU GUYS TO SHOW
YOUR CREATIVE SIDE. NOT ONLY CAN
YOU FORM INTO MUSICAL ACTS,
MAGIC ACTS, BUT YOU CAN ALSO
USE SOUND EFFECTS, LIGHTING,
COSTUMES. LET'S SEE WHAT YOU
COME UP WITH!

This was **AWESOME!** Percy and I already have fartastic superhero costumes, we're great at sound effects (PARFFF!!!) and I'm sure we can invent some very **COOL** stuff for the show.

Mr Hammond also had some . . . errr . . . less good ideas??

. . . AND THIS WILL BE A SPECIAL OPPORTUNITY FOR YOU KIDS TO TEAM UP WITH SOME OF THE KIDS FROM ORCHESTRA.

YOU HEARD RIGHT: ORCHESTRA.

I looked over at Percy and he looked back at me.
I was expecting him to be sick there
and then, but he wasn't. I guess he
didn't understand how pukeworthy the
situation was . . . We were going to
have to team up with the kids from **ORCHESTRA!!**

This was not good news. The kids from orchestra aren't COOL like us kids in science club . . .

They're the **DORKIEST** kids in school! What would they know about **Gross Awful Gasses** and REAL music?! They all play classical music and they . . . well, I don't know what else they do, but whatever it is, it isn't cool like finding COOL STUFF and building things out of FANTASTIC FINDS.

Percy, Superdog and I have just had a special meeting in the secret laboratory (I mean, **CLUBHOUSE**). Some kids in class have started teaming up with some of the kids in orchestra, but Percy and I have hatched a better plan:

With Superdog's help we will form the greatest rock band that the world has ever seen!

We'll have **EXPERIMENTAL FACE** on lead guitar and lead vocals!

 Superdog on backing vocals!

And the AWESOME **Brass Invader** on . . . well . . . everything else!

Ok, we are going to be faced with a couple of challenges. For a start, **Superdog** doesn't exactly pass for a student and he has been permanently banned from school for licking one of Miss Quimby's doughnuts.

Still, Percy and I are masters of disguise, so I'm sure we'll think of something.

One other issue is that we don't have any instruments. Even if we did, we wouldn't know how to play them. Instead, I've had a much better idea — they don't call me a **SUPER AMAZING IMPRESSIVE INVENTOR** for nothing! We will manufacture our own instruments, the likes of which have never been seen!

AND we will name ourselves 'The Farts of
Gratitude' — or FOG, for short.

Percy and I worked on the presentation in our secret laboratory **CLUBHOUSE** for a bit, then we went indoors to have a look on Metal Place to see if anyone had contacted Ms Mills.

We passed the kitchen where Dad was working on his latest invention: fart cola that actually turns your farts **PURPLE**. Dad gave us some to take with us to my room.

We sat down at my desk, turned on my computer, and went to Ms Mills' profile.

There was one message in her inbox:

METAL PLACE DATING

BROFF

I am Broff. I like tanks. Would you like to meet?

ANSWER ➡

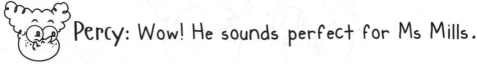

Percy: Wow! He sounds perfect for Ms Mills.

EXCELLENT!! We had one possible victim! I was about to type an answer, but I suddenly

realised we had a bit of a problem. Percy and I were going to have to come up with a way to organise Broff a date with Ms Mills without her finding out:

- THAT SHE WAS ON A DATE

- THAT PERCY AND I HAD ORGANISED THE DATE

Hmmm . . . this was going to require some planning.

I COULD FEEL A GENIUS IDEA BREWING!!!!!

Oh no . . .

. . . it was a **FART** brewing . . .

I thought about it for a while longer and wrote back.

There's been a real buzz at school all week. Some kids have already organised themselves into bands and started rehearsing. Out of all of these, the most ANNOYING by far is smug, full-of-himself, twit-faced Gareth Trumpshaw.

He teamed up with some of the musicians from the orchestra and some kids who sing a capella. He's also got two students from Dance and Drama to help with choreography and he's started — I can hardly bring myself to say it without barfing — a . . . BOY BAND.

You should see them prancing around in the playground surrounded by adoring girls. It's enough to make Percy sick. Actually, I don't know if that counts, it doesn't take a lot to make Percy sick . . . it's enough to make **SUPERDOG** sick!!

He's named the band 'PAST YOUR BEDTIME'. It's the suckiest thing I've ever seen or heard.

To make matters even worse, Gareth's dad has volunteered to help them with the stage show — you know, the sound, the lights, the special effects . . .

A lot of other kids are already rehearsing too:

Nitty Neil and Belinda are practicing **magic tricks.**

Leo and Michael have started hanging around with some kids from orchestra and they're always looking at songs and sheet music.

Amy Almond and Debra Derby keep comparing designs for something or other.

There are kids from every class and every school club dancing, prancing, bouncing, singing . . .

It's a bit like going to school in a CIRCUS (which, by the way, would have been my second choice of school after going to school on a nuclear submarine).

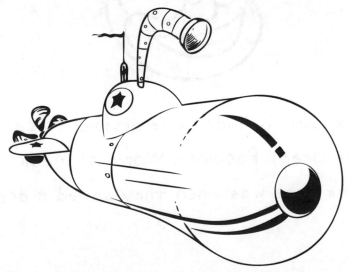

After school, Percy and I made our way to Science Club with our **PRESENTATION**. Mr Hammond had decided to hold our meeting in the school hall as he wanted to see what ideas we'd all come up with. I was sure he wouldn't be disappointed.

Nitty Neil and Belinda have decided to call their act 'The Great Poodini's World of Magic'. My favourite part was when they sawed a dog turd in half.

Gareth and his boyband, **PAST YOUR BEDTIME**, got up and performed a bit of their song 'Don't You Love My Haircut?'. A lot of girls went up to the front of the hall to watch them whilst Percy was being **SICK** in a bin. (Who can blame him? Even I was a bit sick in my mouth.)

Leo and Michael have formed a band called
Diarrhoea Dogs and the Twerking Turds.
They've joined forces with some kids from
Dance and Drama.

The wind section of the orchestra has also got together and formed into a band. They've called themselves 〜 'The Winds of Change'. 〜 Debra Derby and Amy Almond are helping them with their stage design.

A lot of other kids from orchestra presented their ideas. Most of them formed bands (with the exception of two MAGIC ACTS, one contortionist and one mime artist).

Soon it was time for us to present our idea. We hadn't rehearsed anything yet, but we had our presentation ready:

Percy and I would turn into the **MIGHTY EXPERIMENTAL FACE** and the **Relentless Brass Invader** to perform in our **AWESOME** two-man and one-ROBOT (that is, a toad cleverly disguised as a robot) band:

THE FARTS OF GRATITUDE!!!!!

AND UNLIKE ALL THE OTHER BANDS, WE WILL MAKE OUR OWN INSTRUMENTS . . . AND THE ROBOT!

The room fell silent. Clearly everyone was very impressed with the idea and they were all very jealous not to have come up with it.

Mr Hammond looked **REALLY IMPRESSED**, then he said:

'Okay everyone, there are a few kids who haven't thought of anything to do, so we're going to help them find teams.'

He read out a list of students and several kids either happily or begrudgingly joined their teams, then he announced: 'MINA SNOTBRIDGE, with Danny and Percy'.

MINA SNOTBRIDGE

I was stunned! Hadn't Mr Hammond been paying attention? Percy and I had already come up with the **PERFECT** act: The one-man band + lead guitarist + genius toad robot!

Mr Hammond: Okay everyone, this is a great opportunity for you to all make new friends and to learn to work together. I'm sure that there's **LOTS YOU CAN ALL LEARN FROM EACH OTHER!**

Why was he looking at Percy and me?

That's when I realised:

Mr Hammond was just trying to give some lucky student the opportunity to learn from the **BEST**! It would be selfish of Percy and me to keep our genius inventing skills to ourselves.

YES! We would welcome Mina Snotbridge into our inventing team! She would have to swear a vow of secrecy . . .

. . . and sign a confidentiality agreement . . .

. . . and promise to always obey Superdog . . .

. . . but maybe it was time for our WISDOM to be shared.

Mina Snotbridge made her way over to us. She was carrying a big instrument case. I was going to ask what it was, but before I could she said:

IT'S A CELLO. AND I'M MINA.

HI, I'M DANNY. . . THIS IS PERCY.

Hmmm... If Mina Snotbridge could already play an instrument then maybe she could be of some help with the project after all!

Percy, Mina and I arranged to meet at my house on Saturday morning. In the meantime, Percy and I had lots of work to do. Our mission? To hunt high and low in every skip and every dustbin to make the best **FANTASTIC FINDS** for our band projects!

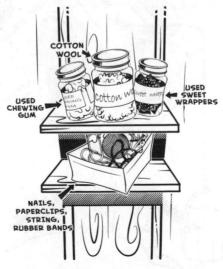

COTTON WOOL

USED CHEWING GUM

USED SWEET WRAPPERS

NAILS, PAPERCLIPS, STRING, RUBBER BANDS

So Saturday morning came around, and by this time Percy and I were prepared to blow Mina Snotbridge away with our ingenious inventions made from our **FANTASTIC FINDS**.

I had made myself a guitar out of:

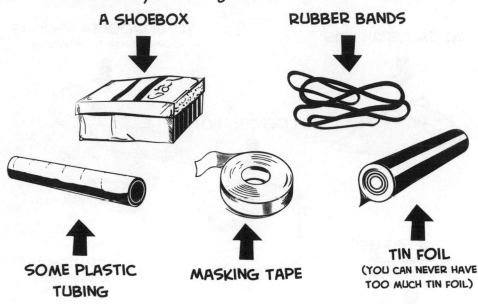

A SHOEBOX

RUBBER BANDS

SOME PLASTIC TUBING

MASKING TAPE

TIN FOIL
(YOU CAN NEVER HAVE TOO MUCH TIN FOIL)

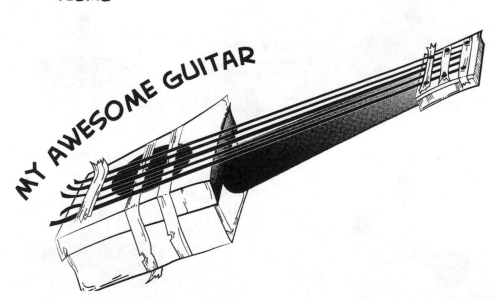

MY AWESOME GUITAR

And Percy made his instrument out of:

TWO SAUCEPAN LIDS

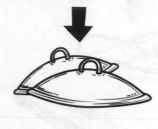

SOME WOODEN SPOONS
(BORROWED FROM THE KITCHEN)

A COOKING POT

A TOILET BRUSH
(BORROWED FROM
THE SCHOOL TOILET)

A HARMONICA
(FOUND IN A DRAIN
BY THE BUS STOP)

A HARNESS
(FOUND ABANDONED NEXT
TO SOME SCAFFOLDING)

A FOG HORN

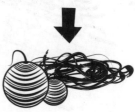

AND LOTS OF WIRE
AND STRING ...

Behold! Percy's **AWESOME** one-man band!!!

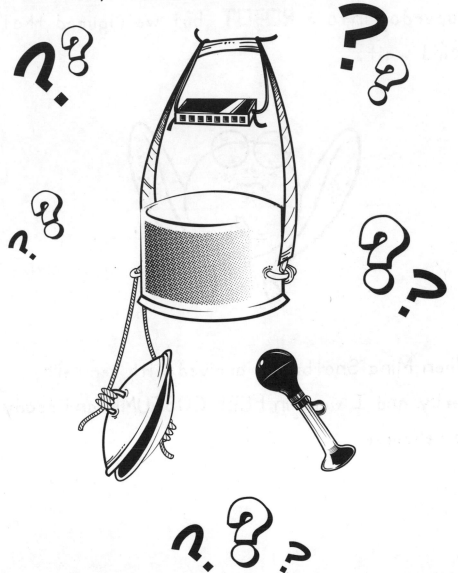

We hadn't quite got round to turning
Superdog into a **ROBOT**, but we figured that
could wait.

When Mina Snotbridge arrived with her cello,
Percy and I were in FULL COSTUME and ready
to rehearse.

Mina climbed up to our clubhouse (cello first) and looked at us, speechless, with her mouth hanging wide open. She was clearly very impressed . . . and she even pretended to be impressed with Percy's costume!

Superdog and I started setting things up and getting ready to teach Mina our song 'Did Something Die In Here?' Mina seemed more interested in getting Percy to show her how his instrument worked.

Dad had been busy experimenting in the kitchen all morning and he kept popping up to the clubhouse wanting us to try a new kind of fart jelly or his latest batch of fart-colouring cola. We were getting nowhere fast was until Mina happened to mention Gareth Trumpshaw's band:

I'VE HEARD THAT GARETH'S BAND HAVE BEEN OFFERED A RECORD DEAL . . .

GARETH IS A TWIT FACE!

AND HIS DAD IS PUTTING TOGETHER THIS REALLY AWESOME STAGE SHOW WITH LASERS AND SMOKE MACHINES . . .

At that point Dad appeared as if from nowhere:

WHAT DID I HEAR YOU SAY . . .? DID YOU SAY THAT GARETH TRUMPSHAW'S DAD IS HELPING HIM CHEAT AGAIN??!!

NO, THAT'S NOT WHAT I . . .

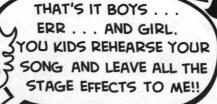

THAT'S IT BOYS . . . ERR . . . AND GIRL. YOU KIDS REHEARSE YOUR SONG AND LEAVE ALL THE STAGE EFFECTS TO ME!!

And with that, Dad vanished from the clubhouse. We could hear him murmuring himself, things like: 'That Trumpshaw twit thinks he can outdo us, does he?' and 'We'll see who has the last laugh!'.

Now, I'm no expert on stage effects, but I know my dad well. Whatever he was planning, it was going to involve fireworks. Fireworks and farting. It was going to be **AWESOME**.

Percy and I spent the rest of the day teaching Mina our **song**. She took lots of notes and promised to rehearse every day.

We arranged to meet up at the same place, same time the following week. This would give Mina time to learn the cello part of the song so we could all rehearse together.

I asked Mina if she could write down the sheet music for the song. She said it would help a lot if Percy went round to her house for extra practice, but I couldn't allow it. Percy and I still had a lot of work to do on **OPERATION FABFART**. Ms Mills had received more messages and we needed to arrange her some dates.

After Mina had left, Percy and I went up to my room, making sure to pick up a little fart jelly on the way past the kitchen.

We went through all of the messages in the inbox we had set up for Ms Mills. There were more than I expected. Percy and I found two more guys that would be perfect: Marcus and Magnus. They both looked a bit like **METAL FACE** (sort of, from a distance) and, most importantly, they both seemed very, very desperate for a girlfriend.

I realised that the most romantic thing we could do for Ms Mills was to get the three candidates to serenade her on public television, by joining our band as backing musicians and playing her our song about farting. I don't know that much about what women like, but if I were a woman I'm sure that this is exactly the sort of thing that I would find really **ROMANTIC**.

Also, having a few people in the band who can play an instrument may help improve our chances of **WINNING** — not that we need much help, our song is a masterpiece ... but we're up against some stiff competition, so it doesn't hurt to have a little extra talent on the team.

I messaged the guys back asking them if they could play any instruments. I saw there was a message from Broff saying that he did like music and that he played the electric guitar. **EXCELLENT**!

So I messaged him back asking if he could learn a song.

The **BIG DAY** is drawing near and everything is falling into place. Mina has prepared the sheet music and we've sent that with the lyrics to our song to Broff, Marcus — who plays the trumpet — and Magnus — who plays the washboard.

I was really looking for two guitarists, a drummer and a bass player, but guitar, trumpet and washboard is close enough.

Percy and I have been helping Mina with her superhero outfit. We found a big roll of **bubble wrap** in the cupboard under the stairs. The rest of the outfit came together easily out of masking tape, two empty cola bottles, an old hanger, a black bin bag for a cape and some cardboard wings with some tin foil.

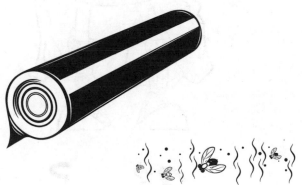

Behold the mysterious **Badger Breath!** (This is just a temporary name until we can come up with something that Mina actually agrees to.)

She did ask a lot of   questions   about why she
had to dress as a superhero, who Broff, Marcus and
Magnus were, what they had to do with Ms Mills,
why we have a toad dressed up as a robot . . .

Eventually I realised that if we wanted Mina's help, we'd have to tell her the truth (sort of).

I told her that our whole act was a cover for a **SPECIAL MISSION:** A mission to get our poor, lonely grumpy teacher a boyfriend to cheer her up.

IT'S CALLED OPERATION FABFA– I MEAN OPERATION CUPID.

AHH! THAT'S SO SWEET!

After Mina had been given official security clearance and received the **CLASSIFIED DETAILS** of our mission she wanted to know a few other things, like how we intended on sneaking three grown adult men onto the stage without Mr Hammond or any of the other teachers noticing.

I had to admit, I hadn't really thought about this . . .

Mina looked over at Percy's one-man band
instrument thingy and then over at Superdog's
cereal-packet-and-tin-foil robot costume . . .
I sensed an air of doubt.

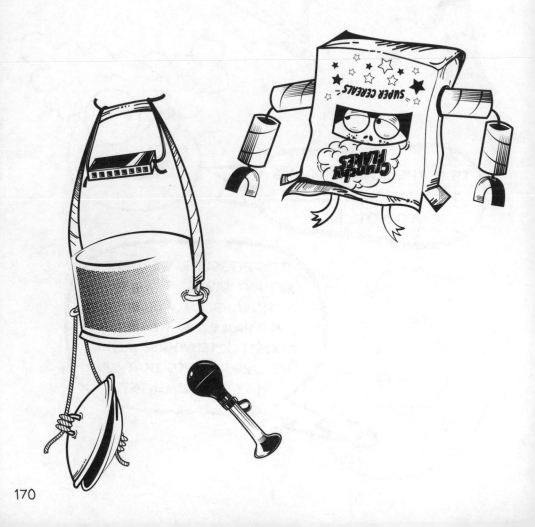

HOW ABOUT WE TELL MR HAMMOND THAT THREE KIDS FROM ORCHESTRA WHO ARE TOO SHY TO COME FORWARD HAVE AGREED TO PLAY THE SHOW WITH US, BUT ONLY IF THEY ARE IN DISGUISE AND NO ONE EVER ASKS FOR THEIR TRUE IDENTITY TO BE REVEALED?

Percy and I looked at each other.

GENIUS!!!

Danny and Percy: Genius!

Percy and I helped Mina out of her **superhero** disguise, then we all went upstairs (stopping by the kitchen to get a bottle of Dad's latest invention — glittery fart cola).

I logged onto the **METAL PLACE DATING** website and messaged Broff, Marcus and Magnus.

MS MILLS

Dear Broff / Marcus / Magnus,
I am really looking forward to seeing you play my favourite song for me live at the school's talent show. I hope you don't mind, but I'd really like it if you dressed up as a superhero when you play the song.
Danny Dingle, the most intelligent and cleverest inventor in school, will help you make an outfit if you need help. He will also be meeting you and playing the song with you. He wrote the song himself, because he is a world-class genius. I will give you Danny's email address so you can get in touch with him from now on. Good luck.
I love you. Ms Mills

Mina and Percy had a look at the email. Percy wasn't happy that he didn't get a mention. Mina seemed to think that it was a bit much to say **"I love you"** at the end. We made some changes:

♥ METAL PLACE DATING

METAL PLACE DATING

MS MILLS

Dear Broff / Marcus / Magnus,
I am really looking forward to seeing you play my favourite song for me live at the school's talent show. I hope you don't mind, but I'd really like it if you dressed up as a superhero when you play the song. Danny Dingle, the most intelligent and cleverest inventor in school, will help you make an outfit if you need help. He will also be meeting you and playing the song with you. He wrote the song himself, because he is a world-class genius AND HIS FRIEND PERCY IS ALSO A WORLD-CLASS GENIUS AND VERY HANDSOME. I will give you Danny's email address so you can get in touch with him from now on. Good luck.
You are nice. Ms Mills

Percy, Mina and I were all set to start designing **superhero** costumes, but all three men messaged back within a few minutes to say that they already had their own hero outfits.

And with that, everything was in place: YAY!
I'd be in contact with Broff, Marcus and Magnus
to arrange for us all to meet just before the
TALENT SHOW for a quick rehearsal.

Mina would be in charge of telling Mr Hammond
that there are three new **BAND MEMBERS**. We
decided to leave it to her as she seems to be
quite good at thinking on her feet.

We've rehearsed the song, Dad
has nearly finished the special
effects, we all have our costumes . . .
we're as ready as we will ever be, and
OPERATION FABFART is on track.
It has been a seamless mission so far and
everything is coming together. The big day
is just around the corner.

In yesterday's assembly everyone was given instructions and stage times for tonight.

The show has to be held on Saturday as apparently it will take all day for the production company to set up all the cameras and lighting. Several people have to go in early to set up **special effects**. Dad is one of them.

The show was going to be held in the gym because the fire wardens had booked the theatre to carry out their annual safety training. **LUCKILY** Mr Hammond managed to get them a new venue two towns away, so we can use the school theatre after all.

The production company have set up **SECURITY** around the theatre to keep out anyone who isn't involved in setting up.

Dad is really chuffed because he's been given a badge saying **'TECHNICAL CREW'**. He spent most of Friday nipping to his car so he could go past security flashing his badge and saying things like 'Special effects technician, coming through'.

Us kids aren't allowed in until this afternoon, so we amused ourselves this morning by hanging out in the car park and farting.

We aren't allowed a full stage rehearsal. Instead, the producer got us all together and told us how we were supposed to go onstage and where to stand. Everything was going to be set up for us just the way we wanted.

We're on at the very end and just after full of himself, twit-faced Gareth Trumpshaw. The producer said that the students who have the MESSIEST special effects go on last so as not to ruin the stage for the following act. I knew she didn't want to tell all the other kids that they were just leaving the BEST till last.

After receiving our instructions, Percy, Mina, Superdog and I went to the car park to wait for Broff, Magnus and Marcus.

We didn't have to wait for long. When we got to the car park we saw a **confused-looking** man standing around wearing a washboard. The other two arrived shortly afterwards.

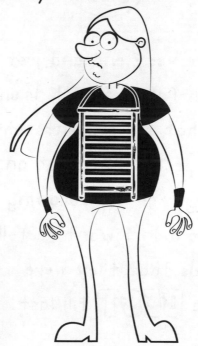

Percy, Mina and I each went to collect a guest. We had a careful script that we had to stick to. It was important that the guys didn't suspect that they were **ALL** there to meet Ms Mills, after all.

This is what we had come up with:

1. We all go onstage and **WOW** Ms Mills with our amazing song, which will leave her speechless and in awe.

2. After the show there's going to be a backstage party. Ms Mills will be there, probably trying to stalk Mr Hammond. After the crowd has finished cheering and we receive our **PRIZE** for being the best act, we'll go to the dressing room.

3. Then I'll take Broff to meet Ms Mills whilst Superdog **HYPNOTISES** Magnus and Marcus. Mina and Percy will keep guard.

4. When I get back, Superdog will hypnotise Broff and wake up Magnus so Percy can take him to Ms Mills. When they get back Superdog will **RE-HYPNOTISE** Magnus and wake up Marcus who'll go with Mina to meet Ms Mills. Simple!

5. When everyone has met Ms Mills, Superdog will hypnotise everyone again whilst we decide who the best boyfriend for Ms Mills is.

6. Then we'll let Superdog wake up the lucky winner. I will take him to Ms Mills and they will fall in love. Ms Mills will be so grateful that I introduced her to the **love of her life** that she'll never make me do P.E. again and, not only will I pass . . . she'll even give me an **A**!

Oh, yeah . . . and I'll tell her that Percy and Mina helped, so they get good grades too.

Everything was set. Mina and Percy knew exactly what they had to do. Mina did object to certain parts of the plan, however, like people having to be hypnotised, people having to be hypnotised by a **TOAD**, and people being **LEFT** hypnotised indefinitely.

We went backstage to get changed and then we had time to watch a few acts so we found some seats at the back of the theatre.

Percy wasn't handling the pressure well so I suggested he should count everyone in the building to calm himself down. When I was little Mum used to ask me to count things like passing cars, or leaves. I still don't know what she needed that information for, but I remember her telling me it was really important. I found it really BRING, but luckily I've got Percy to do that now (he loves counting). Anyway, he ran off leaving Mina and me settled down to scope out our competition.

THE WINDS OF CHANGE had an interesting approach: their song ('Your Wind in My Face') was played with a mixture of wind instruments and farting. The wind instruments were quite loud, so the fart section had to perform bending over with their microphones right by their bums.

After that, Diarrhoea Dog and the Twerking Turds performed their track 'TWERKORREA'. It was good but there was no way it would match us.

LAST NIGHT MY DOG WENT THROUGH THE BINS AND ATE SOME ARTICHOKE, A BALL OF GREASY PAPER AND A USED UP BAR OF SOAP THIS MORNING WE WENT FOR A WALK AND HE WAS OVERCOME HE SPRAYED POO ON THE PAVEMENT WHILST WIGGLING HIS BUM WORK THAT BOOTY, FAR AND NEAR TWERK THAT BOOTY, TWERKORREA . . .

I had to admit, it was pretty catchy. There were a couple more acts after that.

Nitty Neil and Belinda did really well with their act, **The Great Poodini's World of Magic**. It was a welcome change after the previous act . . . Bendy Barbara from year 4, who bit off her own toenails.

I don't think anyone expected what happened next: **Ms Mills** got up onstage with a guitar and dedicated a song to Mr Hammond. The song was called 'I WISH YOU WERE MY TAPEWORM'.

Percy had just finished counting and made it to the front of the stage just as Ms Mills finished her song. The ending was so gross that Percy vomited on the steps up to the stage, which was unfortunate (or not!) as the next band was Gareth Trumpshaw's boyband, **PAST YOUR BEDTIME**.

All the members of **PAST YOUR BEDTIME** had to walk through Percy's sick and, well . . . one thing led to another . . .

BLEURGH!

A few of the backing dancers just couldn't stand the smell and were sick on stage. It was a bit of a chain reaction: one dancer was sick, another dancer slipped and fell in it . . . then that dancer was sick.

Basically Gareth's act consisted of a bunch
of kids in neon lycra throwing up and slipping
around in their own sick. It was much better
than I'd expected. Gareth looked mortified
throughout the whole act.

At one point I could swear he looked towards us
mouthing the words "I'll get you for this". . .
but I could be wrong. I just smiled and gave him
a big thumbs up.

I really thought Gareth was going to cry at the end . . . until all the kids in the audience got up and clapped. I wasn't expecting that, and neither was Gareth from the look on his face.

This was going to make them a **VERY DIFFICULT** act to follow.

Anyway, there was a short break as the organisers decided that there was just a bit too much **SICK** on the stage for the next act to go on.

BLEURGH!

At this point it was time to hit the dressing rooms and finish getting ready. Mina had got backstage passes for Broff, Magnus and Marcus. As for Superdog, I had managed to ingeniously smuggle him past security by hiding him in a large box of doughnuts. **ALTHOUGH** I didn't like the look we got from Miss Quimby. A box of **DOUGHNUTS** is never safe if she's anywhere nearby.

Broff said he'd meet me in the dressing room because he had to go to his car and get his superhero disguise and guitar. I made my way to the dressing room to meet up with Mina, Percy, Magnus, Marcus and Superdog.

Magnus and Marcus had already changed. Unfortunately they'd both decided to wear **METAL FACE** costumes, which was extremely **COOL**, but it also made it a little difficult to tell them apart. We'd just have to hope that Magnus kept his guitar on him at all times and Marcus kept hold of his trumpet . . . or was Marcus the one with the washboard?

As this thought was going through my head
Broff walked through the dressing room door.
He had already changed . . . into his Metal Face
costume. Percy, Mina and I looked at each
other. It was going to be VERY difficult to
tell them apart. We'd just have to hope that
Superdog followed through with his part of the
plan.

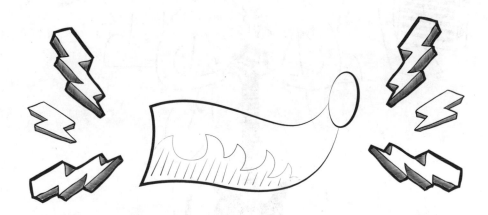

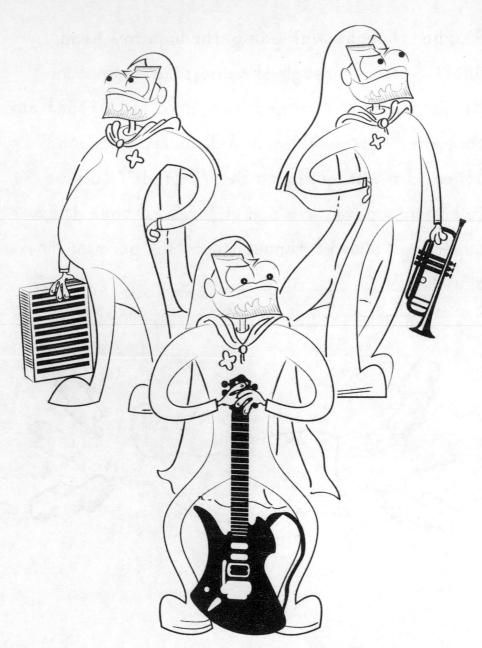

I looked over at the table where Superdog . . .
WASN'T!!! Where was he? I started sending him
telepathic signals: 'Superdog . . . come back and get
ready to hypnotise our musicians!'. No messages back.

I panicked! All was lost! Suddenly I heard a splosh
and . . . PHEW!! Superdog was sloshing around in
a bucket of paint that the school had used for the
set. His costume was all soggy (and bright red),
but there was no time to worry about that.

I'd just rescued Superdog from his bath when there was a knock on the door: 'Farts of Gratitude . . . you're on!'.

This was it, the moment we had all been waiting for. We all looked at each other thinking the exact same thing and knowing exactly what we had to do.

We left the safety of the dressing room and took our positions **ONSTAGE**. I looked over at Dad who was standing just off the stage behind the curtains and he gave me an excited thumbs up.

I looked ahead into the audience, but I couldn't really see much as I was blinded by the stage lights. I approached the mic. This was a lot of pressure, but I could deal with it . . . **EXPERIMENTAL FACE** can deal with anything!

I took a deep breath and announced: 'Good evening people! We are the **FARTS OF GRATITUDE!**' I was interrupted by a big cheer. 'Thank you, thank you. This is a song we'd like to dedicate to someone very special who's here tonight. Ms Mills, this song's for you.'

DID YOU THROW OUT THE RUBBISH?
IS SOMETHING CLOGGING UP THE SINK?
COULD IT BE A ROTTEN ONION?
SOMEONE TELL ME, WHAT'S THAT STINK?
HAS THE CAT GONE AND FARTED?
DOES IT HAVE DIARRHOEA?
HAS THE SOCK PILE GONE MOULDY?
OR HAS SOMETHING DIED IN HERE?

SOMETHING IS DECOMPOSING,
IT MIGHT BE UNDER THE BED

BETTER GET A STICK TO PROD IT,
COS I'M PRETTY SURE IT'S DEAD

IT COULD BE THE NEXT-DOOR NEIGHBOUR,
MAKING CABBAGE CASSEROLE

IS SHE TRYING A NEW RECIPE?
PICKLED ONION-FLAVOURED TROLL?

SOMETHING IS DECOMPOSING,
IT MIGHT BE UNDER THE BED

BETTER GET A STICK TO PROD IT,
COS I'M PRETTY SURE IT'S DEAD

BETTER OPEN A WINDOW,
AND JUST LET IN A BREEZE
COS THIS WHOLE PLACE JUST SMELLS
LIKE CRUSTY ARMPITS AND CHEESE

SOMETHING IS DECOMPOSING!
IT MIGHT BE UNDER THE BED
BETTER GET A STICK TO PROD IT,
COS I'M PRETTY SURE IT'S DEAD

I could just about make out Ms Mills' face in the audience. She looked impressed . . . really, really impressed . . . then she came a little closer and I could see that impressed wasn't really the word. She looked ANGRY . . . really, **REALLY ANGRY.**

She seemed to be stomping towards the stage in a very **SCARY** sort of way.

Broff made a brave dash for the front of the stage where he started knocking out this fantastic guitar solo to impress Ms Mills, but then Percy's one-man band contraption got tangled up in Broff's guitar lead.

I looked over at Dad and signalled for him to set off some effects. Hopefully he could set off a smokescreen that would allow us all to escape backstage before Ms Mills could get to Percy. Dad started randomly pushing buttons on a hand-held controller, setting off cannons of **GLITTER**.

As Ms Mills started climbing onto the stage, Dad managed to set off the **SMOKE MACHINES**, which he had modified slightly by adding curried broccoli fart aroma into the mix. It was nauseating, even if I do say so myself.

In all the confusion and smoke I heard Percy being sick . . . and I heard someone who sounded a lot like Ms Mills screaming in horror. I put two and two together, and worked out that this was not going to be good for Percy.

I'd made it backstage safely and so had Mina, but Percy was still onstage tangled up in Broff's guitar lead.

I peeked my head around the curtains in time to witness Ms Mills screaming at the musicians: 'What on Earth do you think you're doing? I smell nothing like pickled-onion-flavoured troll!'.

The musicians had all rallied around Ms Mills now, eager to declare their love . . .

At this point the guys didn't look happy. They weren't really focused on Ms Mills anymore: they looked more focused on starting a FIGHT.

Percy sensed the danger and rolled off the front of the stage onto Dad, who accidentally pushed all the buttons on his controller and set off all the remaining **SPECIAL EFFECTS** at the same time.

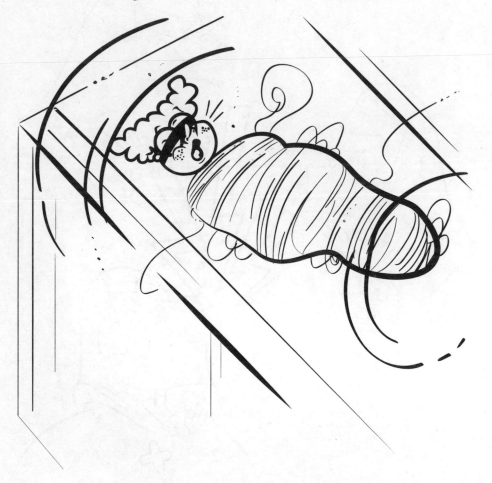

As the fart cannons set off blasts of cabbage casserole fart and **BAKED BEAN TREMBLER**, the audience started coughing, heaving and running out screaming. This was definitely for the best as the three musicians were now rolling around onstage beating each other up. Meanwhile, Percy had managed to roll into Dad's **confetti launchers**, causing them to fire off in random directions.

Suddenly there was a thud and a really big bang which took everyone by surprise. Tons of confetti started raining down and the stage area started to fill with really thick **smoke**.

There was a crackling from the P.A. system, then we all heard Gareth Trumpshaw's weasly voice saying:

Gareth: Evacuate, evacuate! This is an emergency! Danny Dingle and his father have set the stage on fire, run for your lives!

There was a stampede as people scrambled for the closest exit. It was a bit like the January sales, except everyone was trying to get OUT of the building.

I realised I had to get out of there. I rushed backstage and found Mina.

My heart sank.

Mina and I looked everywhere we could think of, but Superdog was nowhere to be found.

Soon we were the only two people left in the building, so Mina grabbed me by the hand and dragged me outside.

I looked around. Everyone seemed to have made it out alive. Dad was trying to **untangle** Percy from the guitar lead he was still wrapped in.

Mr Hammond and the producer turned to look at my dad.

Mr Hammond: If you're responsible for this, James Dingle, the school will come down on you like a ton of bricks.

Producer: Yes, what kind of person brings fireworks into a school?

I didn't want to say anything. Dad had had a few incidents with fireworks in the past . . . like the time he accidentally burnt down the factory where he was working.

Dad: What are you talking about? This wasn't my fault! I didn't take fireworks into the theatre — or anything else that could start a fire — you have the wrong man!

Mr Hammond and the producer looked unconvinced. I have to admit that even I had my doubts.

Mr Hammond: Did everyone get out alive? How can we know if anyone is missing?

Producer: We don't have a head count.
Just then a freshly untangled Percy butted in.

PERCY COUNTED EVERYONE EARLIER. HE'S REALLY GOOD AT IT.

THE ONLY PERSON I CAN'T SEE IS SUPERDO- I MEAN, OUR ROBOT.

DON'T WORRY PERCY, IT WAS ONLY A ROBOT. YOU CAN ALWAYS MAKE ANOTHER.

Percy and I looked at each other and my eyes filled with tears.

SUPERDOG!!! WHY?????

You were too young to die, too clever, too good looking . . .

AAAAGHHHH!!!!

Suddenly we heard a very loud, somewhat familiar SCREAM. We turned around in time to see Miss Quimby faint as she dropped a box of doughnuts . . . and there, in the middle, covered in powdered sugar and paint was **SUPERDOG**!!!

Dad stood with Mr Hammond and the producer as they waited for the police to come and question Dad. But as the smoke began to clear we saw that the school theatre was still standing. There wasn't any sign of a fire anywhere.

Dad: What's going on? I thought you said the theatre was on fire?

Mr Hammond: I never said I saw a fire . . .

Producer: Who said they'd seen a fire?

We all turned to look at smug, full-of-himself, twit-faced Gareth Trumpshaw. . .

Gareth: What? You can't blame me for thinking that Mr Dingle would start a fire. I mean, there was smoke . . . no smoke without fire, right?

I couldn't believe it! Gareth had made the whole thing up to get back at me over the ACCIDENT with the sick!

It turns out that all that had happened was that one of the **confetti** canons had fired sideways and set one of the smoke machines off on full power. There was no fire and there was no smoke! It was all dry ice!

All the adults headed back towards the theatre to start clearing up. Percy, Mina, Superdog and I sat together on the pavement by the car park. Yes, there may have been a few MINOR disasters, but all in all it had been quite a good afternoon.

Unfortunately, Ms Mills didn't seem even remotely interested in any of her possible boyfriends. It probably didn't help that they were all gathered in a corner covered in bruises. But at least she wasn't stalking Mr Hammond. Instead she seemed to be trying to flirt with a fireman.

I thought that at least I should go and speak to Broff, Marcus and Magnus.

I made my way over to them, ready to apologise for Ms Mills' shocking behaviour.

Broff: Hey dude, **AWESOME** gig!

Magnus: Yeah man, that was epic!

Marcus: My favourite bit was the fight.

Then Broff said something REALLY inte

Broff: Never mind, the producer just came to talk to us and she said she was really impressed with our act. She wants to hire us as a backing band for some famous act . . . are you guys in?

I looked over at Percy, Superdog and Mina . . . the offer was tempting, but I knew that our fate was to keep inventing. Metal Face needed us . . . even if he didn't know it yet.

Danny: That's okay, you guys go ahead. We have fantastic finds to make and world-class inventions to invent.

off: Okay, that's cool. By the way, I think the producer wanted to speak to you about buying your song. She really liked it and she says it would be perfect for this famous band she's been working with!

She had a point: it was probably one of the best things I had **EVER** come up with. But the world needed our song. I couldn't keep it to myself.

Danny: Don't you see, Mina? It is our mission to get everybody to rock out! If my — OUR — song can help to do that, then I have to let it go! . . . AND the money could come in very handy for this new invention I've been thinking about . . .

Last night was great! Mina and Percy came round to my house so we could all watch the screening of:

This School Has
★✦ Talent ✦★
WHEN THINGS
GO WRONG!

The TV show producers had been in touch with the school to say that the event had been the worst display of disorganisation, horrible songs and general chaos they'd ever seen. They thought it would make a great **TV SPECIAL** and they paid the school a lot of money for the footage.

There was also going to be a very special **SURPRISE PERFORMANCE** before of the talent show.

And when we tuned in, there they were:

Metal Face wearing his **AWESOME** super-squirter sun hat (patent pending) . . . and his new backing band. I couldn't believe it! There they were, Broff, Magnus and Marcus playing in **Gross Awful Gasses**! And EVEN better, they were performing ~~my~~ our song 'Did Something Die In Here?'. It was AWESOME!!!

And everyone in the audience was rocking out!

MISSION ACCOMPLISHED!!!